Spread
Your
Wings

Spread Your Wings

Steven Dumar

For Marie

"Hope is the thing with feathers that perches in the soul —
and sings the tunes without the words
— and never stops at all."

Emily Dickinson

At the bottom of a long sloping garden stood a large aviary housing a flock of ninety-two African-Grey parrots, the private collection of a private man.

The cage — known to the resident birds as 'Avalona' — was twenty feet long by twenty feet wide by twenty feet high. A perfect box. In the centre stood a solitary synthetic mango tree bearing fake leaves and plastic fruit. Wooden bird boxes with corrugated tin roofs lined the branches and feeders hung from twigs. An array of toys dangled from the tree's limbs — slides, swings, hoops, and rings. A welcome distraction from their forced labour.

Wings are for working. Twines of rope were festooned from branch to branch creating a complex network of bridges and pulleys that transported the parrots around the enclosure, as after many generations of captivity, corruption and conditioning, they had long since lost the ability of flight.

The morning alarm rang. A high-pitched screeching blasted around Avalona, jarring the birds awake. Time for work.

Puck stirred in his nest, covering his ears with cupped wings to muffle the incessant shrieking. He peeled open his eyes and stared vacantly at the ceiling. His dark pupils had once radiated with curiosity and wonder but were now faded into a hollow void as if a light from within had been switched off long ago. He blinked and broke into an exaggerated yawn whilst stretching out his impressive wingspan. *Another day in paradise,* he grumbled before reluctantly rolling out of his nest and moping over to the toy mirror in the corner. His reflection displayed a plumage of ashen grey feathers against a striking red tail.

His beak was curved and as sharp as his mind. He poked out a clay tongue and began routinely licking himself clean when the alarm sounded again, so Puck cut short his preening ritual and went on his way to work.

The thriving metropolis of Avalona had come alive. Flocks of Greys emerged from their boxes. Mother hens shooed their offspring to school whilst couples pecked each other on the cheek before departing on their daily commute, erupting into a raucous cacophony of shrills, squawks, chirps, cheeps, whooping whistles and bleating beeps.

Puck squeezed through his round door and grasped onto Branch Thirteen — the lowest rung of the tree — where the lower-class citizens dwelled. An icy wind blasted through the bars and whipped round the cage, nearly knocking him off his branch. He dug into the artificial bark, his scaly claws curled over like reptilian toes, then glanced down at the concrete floor. On ground level was a faux-marble birdbath where the wealthy and influential went to relax and discuss important matters. And right at the bottom of the aviary, those without a box roamed the fringes, outcast from society and caked in avian activity, hoping for scraps to fall from above. The wind picked up, carrying the festering stench of damp sawdust and rotten droppings.

"Good morning, Puck."

Startled, he looked up to see his neighbour, Rita, an elderly hen who lived on Branch Twelve. She was stood proudly on her perch, the gust blowing her feathers sideways. Her plumes were a duller shade of grey and her red tail had faded after many tough years of cage life.

"Morning Rita."

"Another day in paradise," she chirped.

"Another day in paradise," he repeated as any respectable parrot should.

"It's blowing a hooley! You best be careful up there."

"Will do Rita. And on that note, I should get going. Major Gruber said if I'm late once more, he'll toss me in the Coop."

They both flinched and looked out at the

far reaches of Avalona, beyond the birdbath, where tucked away in the shadows stood an old chicken house fortified with razor-sharp wire and repurposed into a prison. A cage within a cage. Any bird caught defying Queen Bola's regime was thrown in the Coop, never to be seen again.

"Alright then dear, best be off then," said Rita waving him goodbye before heading off to work herself despite being well past the age of retirement.

Cautiously Puck shuffled along the branch, fighting the squall until he reached the centre, where wooden pegs formed a spiral staircase snaking around the trunk. He hopped up the steps until running into a queue of gridlocked parrots. Rush hour traffic. There was little-to-no movement, the line dribbling forward as workers branched off to their respective offices. A group of midwives stepped onto Branch Nine and 'The Hatchery', a communal nest where eggs were laid, incubated, and hatched — baby chicks born into this utopian reality.

The line trickled along. Puck grew impatient,

fidgeting and clawing at his scalp. He passed Branch Seven and his former school, where infants went to be educated about the wide world of Avalona. As impressionable fledglings, they learned all the necessary requirements to become a well-adjusted member of the cage. They'd discovered how their flock had descended from the divine dodo, their direct ancestors, with the Avalonians part of the famous flightless family, distant cousins of the ostrich and penguin. In class, they were repeatedly warned about the dangers of 'The Outside World' that lay beyond the bars. A place of unspeakable horror, where carnivores hid round corners, savages lurked in the shadows, and predators swooped from the skies, ready to pounce on the poor flightless parrots.

As more workers branched off the pace picked up and Puck reached the lofty heights of Branch Three. Here, in the tree's upper echelons, affluent birds resided in their big fancy boxes. He'd promised himself that one day he'd become successful and move up here with the other high-flyers. However, since leaving school and entering the 'Real World', he had worked non-stop yet was still struggling to make ends meet down there with the others. At the very top of the tree stood the Royal Palace, a grand box inhabited by Queen Bola, supreme leader of Avalona. Equally loved and feared, the monarch was a formidable ruler with an iron wing, notorious for incarcerating unruly citizens. She was protected by a troop of Patrol Guards, loyal henchmen who roamed the cage ensuring laws were upheld and rules followed. *Wings are for working.* As expected, Queen Bola emerged from the palace surrounded by an entourage of Patrol Guards and took her rightful position on the Royal Perch, overlooking her subjects.

Puck eventually reached his workstation on Branch Two. The Watchtower was a box much larger than his own with a rectangular window for observation, striking a resemblance to a bird-watching hut. Before entering he peeped inside, then over his shoulder to make sure nobody saw him arrive. The place appeared empty, so he slipped in and crept along the floor.

"You're late Corporal!"

His feathers stood on edge. Busted. He sheepishly turned round and saluted his superior, who just about managed to squeeze through the door. Major Gruber was an imposing bird who towered over him in size and stature. His presence filled the Watchtower. Puck shuffled his feet and spoke in an apologetic tone.

"Sorry sir, the traffic—"

"Poppycock!" spat Major Gruber in his clipped voice, pencil moustache bristling above his bill. "This is the third time you've been late this month."

"But—"

"No buts Corporal. There comes a time in a Grey's life when he must stop blaming the world and start taking responsibility for his actions." The Major took a measured pause, allowing the words to linger in the air for dramatic effect. "See that tag on your leg?"

Puck looked down at the orange tag clipped above his left claw. "Yes Sir."

"That tag is a badge of honour. A symbol

of our liberty. Proud to be born and raised as a citizen of Avalona. This place is paradise for parrots. A perfectly functioning society of law and order." Major Gruber spread his wings open in full embrace of the aviary. "Our dodo ancestors fought and died for this freedom, so you could live here in privilege with feed in your beak and a roof over your head. I will not jeopardise the well-being of our residents by leaving them in the wings of a lazy, incompetent parrot who can't be bothered to get out of his nest in the morning. Punctuality is paramount."

"Yes sir."

"Good. Now, see those bars?"

Puck looked at the gridded metal mesh encompassing them. "Sir."

"Those glorious bars protect us by preventing attacks from the Outside World." The Major winced at the words as if they would bring a curse upon his flock. "Life out *there* is evil. You hear me, corporal? EVIL! Teeming with barbarians waiting to devour us delicious parrots. Remember your training: '*An attack is always imminent, so a Lookout Guard must always be vigilant'*. The evil out there never rests, so neither should you."

"Yes sir."

"This is your final warning. Stroll in late once more and you're in the Coop. I mean it this time. Do you understand the words coming out of my rostrum?"

"Sir, yes sir."

"Good. Now get to work."

They gave their salutations then Major Gruber marched off in a huff and Corporal Puck assumed his duties, taking his position on the Lookout Perch. He stared beyond the bars and into the Outside World where the same old daily scene unfolded. The view from his window directly faced a pond that played host to a range of devious fowl. A mob of shady ducks squabbled on the surface, bickering in garish quacks. At the water's edge, scheming pigeons bobbed suspiciously back and forth, plotting and pecking away, waiting to seize their opportunity. A gang of seagulls circled above as shifty sparrows practiced their attacking formations. No direct threats detected, yet.

The morning shift passed without incident as always. Growing restless, Puck gnawed his tail and plucked his feathers. The pain of ripping plume from flesh a temporary release from the boredom. It was unnatural for a parrot to spend such a long time standing stationary and solitary. Empty thunder rumbled in his gut as he fantasized about food when right on cue the 'Featherless One' appeared. An old man wearing green dungarees, Wellington boots, and a straw hat hobbled down the garden path battling the wind and holding buckets of feed. Lunchtime. The Lookout Guard gave the signal and a guttural squawk bellowed around Avalona. Instantly the birds dropped their tasks and stood at attention as The Featherless One approached, fumbling with a set of keys, oblivious to the enclosure's inner workings.

The door creaked open, and the domesticated servant entered without bothering to close it behind him. Silent anticipation filled the aviary. Nobody moved a feather.

A wooden ladder rested against an interior wall. All eyes followed the Featherless One as he placed it against the trunk and started climbing, humming a monotonous tune whilst stopping to check water levels and sweep out boxes. The parrots laboured to maintain formation. From afar Puck observed this strange creature. Its youthful blue eyes contrasted with the cobweb of wrinkles that surrounded them. The plumes on its head were wispy and white, a coy smile etched across its wizened beakless face. It reached Branch Thirteen and refilled the feeder outside Puck's box. He struggled to suppress an itch that had broken out over his recently plucked skin, but it was hopeless. The Taxman would claim most of his rations before he even got home.

Beaks salivated as the Featherless One continued replenishing supplies, emptying the remaining contents of its bucket into Queen Bola's feeder. Not that it made much difference. Her regime would claim most of the taxed rations in any case. Having finished its rounds, the Featherless One descended the ladder, rested it against the wall, and said goodbye.

The door slammed with a definitive thud.

Excitement gripped Avalona. Like a hawk, Corporal Puck watched the servant shuffle up the path. As soon as it was out of sight, he gave the signal and chaos ensued. Pandemonium. The famished parrots erupted into a frenzy of beak and feather. Puck exited the Watchtower onto Branch Two, where a pair of Patrol Guards were already shovelling feed into their gobs. Being lower in the pecking order, the corporal waited for his turn, until the Patrol Guards were satisfied. Stuffed to the brim, they rubbed their potbellies and trotted off leaving only measly crumbs. Puck disappointedly inspected the pithy amount by poking out his tongue and flicking specks into his bill like a croupier dealing cards. The mixture of seed tasted insipid, though the young parrot didn't know any better. After the last grain had been finished, he returned to work.

A diligent rhythm overcame the enclosure as they settled into their quotidian duties like a hive of honeybees. The afternoon shift dragged, as always. No threats detected. It had started to rain. Puck listened to raindrops pitter-pattering off the tin roof whilst staring wistfully into the Outside World. He gazed skywards at the dull blanket of grey stretching over the horizon. 'Just like me', he lamented, letting out an extended sigh as if releasing stale air from a tyre. He wondered if there was more to life than 'this' — this job, this cage, this routine. The futile mundanity of it all. Thoughts flashed through his mind, flights of fancy, crazy notions about a whole world out there, waiting to be discovered. As his imagination drifted to what lay beyond the bars a yearning washed over him, a longing he couldn't quite place. Then the alarm rang. Home-time.

Workers returned to their boxes to settle in for the evening and recharge their batteries for the following day. Puck left the Watchtower and filed into formation, following the flow of traffic down the spiral pegs until reaching Branch Thirteen. He climbed into his box, crawled into his nest and fell into a dreamless sleep.

Winter rolled into spring. The longer days

meant extended working hours. Time merged into one homogenised blur: work, eat, sleep, repeat. Puck had stopped daydreaming about what lay beyond the bars and turned his attentions to getting a promotion. Major Gruber had promised him that if he put his beak down, worked hard, and stopped asking so many questions he could rise to the rank of sergeant, which would include perks such as extra feed and moving to a bigger box on a higher branch. Like an obedient parrot Puck obliged, slowly working his way into the Major's favour by going above and beyond in his line of duty, even snuffing out a potential coup by a pair of rogue pigeons. He was becoming a valuable member of society, a vital cog in the machine, a rising star with a promising future.

The morning alarm rang. Puck awoke and went to work. He entered the Watchtower and stood on the Lookout Perch. Outside, the same old scene unfolded: ducks quacked, pigeons cooed, seagulls cawed. No threats detected. *Another day in paradise.* The morning shift came and went, as did the Featherless One. Lunchtime slipped by too fast, and the afternoon dragged on too slow. He stared absently into space, his thoughts drifting between feed and sleep and back again into nothingness. The more time that drifted away the more Puck felt detached, further removed from life inside and outside Avalona. Clouds turned a darker shade of grey as day morphed into dusk. Yet another tedious shift was coming to end. He was about to clock off when he spied something in the distance that piqued his interest. An unfamiliar sight. In the semi-darkness he couldn't quite make out its shape, but as it drew closer a clearer picture came into focus. A swarm of screeching birds. Thousands of them flashed across the purple sky, moving as one collective mind, contorting this way and that in intricate swirling patterns, punctuating the dusky backdrop like a smudged thumbprint.

Puck stood on high alert, captivated yet conflicted, unsure if this shrieking flock were a divine message or a threat to national security. Were they angels or devils? He went to cry out the war signal but couldn't move, couldn't take his eyes from the murmuration majestically dancing through pockets of violet clouds like a troupe of winged ballerinas. Mesmerised, he remained rooted to the spot, beak agape in awe, lost in rapture. His feathers stood on end as if electrified goosebumps. Powerful currents washed over his body, pulsating to the tips of his wings, coursing through his spirit, elevating him higher and higher until he became one with their motions — spinning and twirling and twisting and swirling through an infinite expanse of sky.

Then just like that the flock vanished. Normality returned as if nothing extraordinary had happened. The other parrots appeared either ignorant or oblivious to the natural wonder that'd just spontaneously unfolded before them. Most had already returned to their boxes without a murmur of excitement, ready to turn in for the evening and do it all again tomorrow.

Puck remained on the Lookout Perch until the sky had turned black. Exhilarated, every atom in his being hummed with life as if a dormant superpower had been awakened. He stared at his wings like never before, folding them round and round in figures of eight whilst repeating aloud the words, "I can fly...I can fly..." At first the statement sounded ridiculous, but the more he repeated the words the more he believed them.

It was the early hours when Puck exited The Watchtower. Outside everything was still and silent. He skipped down the stairs two pegs at a time, floating, yet also wary not to get caught breaking curfew. He slipped inside his box, leapt into his nest and stared at the ceiling, panting excitedly, pupils dilating like flying discs, his mind racing with so many questions and possibilities. He was *awake*.

Wide-eyed, the parrot lay there all night until the first light broke. That magical twilight hour between night and dawn when the nocturnal beasts have returned to their dark holes and the impending glimmer brings promise of a new day. Puck hopped out of his nest and went to the window. In the faint distance he could hear the morning song of skylarks. He perched there for an eternity, basking in their concerto, their alluring melodies serenading his soul. He'd heard their songs before, like background noise filling in the silence, but he'd never truly *listened*.

Then the alarm pierced through the cage. Time for work.

"Early bird catches the worm," said Major Gruber as the corporal entered the Watchtower. "Glad you could make it on time"

"Yes sir."

The Major stroked his beak, squinting with one eye. "So, what happened last night then?"

The question caught Puck off guard. His mind flashed back to the thousands of birds lighting up the sky in fluid rippling patterns, and the powerful sensations that erupted through his body. He felt a slight flickering in his wings but decided to play dumb.

"Last night, sir?"

"Yes, last night. You see corporal, as Lookout Guard of Avalona the sole purpose of your existence is to sound the alarm when a potential threat has been identified."

"Threat sir?"

"Don't give me that tosh!" shouted the Major, spit flying from his bill. "Did you not see that great flock of wild birds?"

"Ahh yes sir, I did."

"And yet I didn't hear any alarm. Not so much as a peep, which put our residents in grave danger."

"But nothing happened—"

"That's immaterial Corporal. You're well on your way to becoming a sergeant, so shape up! Should that situation occur again sound the alarm, understood?"

"Yes sir."

"Good. Now back to work."

They gave their salutations. Major Gruber was about to leave when Puck called out, "Sir!"

The Major spun on his heels and raised an eyebrow. "Yes?"

The young Grey took a nervous moment before speaking. "Last night sir, I felt a strange tingling in my body."

"Perfectly natural for a parrot of your age," he replied without missing a beat.

Confused, Puck tilted his head to one side, "But what were those things?"

"Starlings," he spat with venomous contempt. "Migrating east."

"Why don't we migrate sir?"

"Because we can't fly," stated the Major matter-of-factly.

Puck had heard this fact repeated since he'd hatched. It had been drummed into his skull every single day. Regurgitated. But it no longer rang true. Parrots could fly. He *knew* it. He could feel it in the fibre of his wings. He then asked the same question he'd posed since he was a chick but without ever receiving a satisfactory answer.

"But why can't we fly, sir?"

"Didn't you learn anything in school?" The Major sneered with intellectual superiority, then repeated the lines as if reading from an auto-cue. "We are descendants of the divine dodo. Distant relatives to the penguin and ostrich. Distinct members of the famous flightless family."

"I know, sir, that's what we learnt. But don't you ever get the feeling you can fly?"

The Major's stern face softened into a patronising smirk, "Flying parrots?" he mocked. "That's the most preposterous thing I've ever heard. Our wings are made for working, not flying. So, on that note corporal, pipe down and get on with your job."

"Yes sir."

"And I don't want to ever hear any more of this nonsense. That kind of talk could land you in the Coop...or worse...understood?"

"Sir yes sir!"

Major Gruber disappeared. Puck stepped onto the Lookout Perch and stared into the Outside World, but with a new set of eyes. He observed the wild birds through a different lens. His attention was drawn to some ducks. They'd once appeared so hostile, squabbling in their rowdy quacks, but they now seemed playful and joyous, splashing about the lily pads. These fowls no longer appeared as foes. Then he spotted a flock of sparrows. As he followed them flitting from tree to tree the conditioning melted away. Tranquillity replaced anxiety. They no longer seemed a threat to national security. They didn't appear to be planning an invasion or conspiring to conquer Avalona, as he'd been led to believe. In fact, they seemed disinterested in the cage altogether. Even the pigeons appeared indifferent. Puck used to feel pity for those poor savages, trapped out there, fending for themselves, fighting for every scrap. Now he felt envy. He wanted what they had. Freedom.

Nothing made sense anymore. Avalona had once seemed enormous, so full of promise and opportunity. Now it felt cramped, filthy, and squalid. He stopped looking through the bars and instead stared at them. For the first time, he considered the possibility they'd been put there not to prevent birds from coming in, but to stop them from getting *out*. The longer he pondered this notion, the more it made sense. Dots connected as he pieced together the lie of his life. Then it all unravelled, like a magician pulling back the veil to reveal the trick. A cruel, sick joke. In that moment his whole reality flipped upside-down and inside-out. Everything was backward. Everything he'd ever known to be true came crashing down, engulfing him in meshed steel. The walls closed in. Confining. Constricting. Suffocating.

The day burnt by in a haze of indignation. Puck couldn't stand still. He was seething, pacing round the Watchtower, starkly aware of his captivity and mad at the world. He felt naïve for having been duped, disillusioned at his fellow birds for being so submissive, and consumed by a rampant desire to break free of this hellish existence.

Darkness descended on Avalona. The residents finished their duties and headed home. Puck filed into line and followed the flock. He climbed into his box but refused to crawl into his nest. Instead, he bided his time, waiting for the others to fall asleep. Once their snores could be heard rising and falling in undulating waves, he seized his opportunity. He poked his head outside to check nobody was there, careful not to get caught breaking curfew. Satisfied the coast was clear, he snuck onto Branch Thirteen. As it was the lowest branch, it seemed a good place to start learning how to fly.

He loosened his grip on the bark, closed his eyes, and jumped.

He didn't even flap, just held out his wings and plunged through the air like a pebble, then hit the concrete floor with a thud.

Sprawled on his back, Puck felt a slicing through his skull and a dull throbbing shot up his spine. His tail was crushed. He forced open his eyes and gazed beyond the cage ceiling. The mercurial glow of a full moon hung in the night sky, illuminating a canvas of stars. He'd always wondered what they were, those millions of flickering beacons underpinning the cosmos. When he was a chick, he used to claim that he would one day fly to each one. That notion was soon beaten out of him. *Wings are for working.*

Renewed by feelings of injustice, he got to his feet, brushed himself down, and jumped again. This time he leapt with gusto but crashed once more. The third attempt he made a pathetic effort at flapping, and crashed yet again, though had managed to land into a forward roll, which softened the blow physically but not emotionally.

He hunched over, panting and perplexed, lost in a world of pain and confusion. He'd been convinced parrots could fly, but now swathes of doubt clouded his mind. "This is silly," he muttered, "What am I doing?" Overcome with humiliation, Puck decided to cut his losses and return home to ponder his next move.

Spring blossomed into summer. The days got longer which meant working hours were extended further, but nobody seemed to notice, nobody seemed to care. The Greys just put their heads down and got on with it. All the promises of promotion and pay rise failed to materialise, though Puck wasn't too bothered. Undiscouraged by his initial attempts at flight, he continued to practice in the grips of night, with similarly disappointing results, and bearing the scars to prove it. Following a nasty fall he'd broken a wing in two places, so had taken time out to recover. After a stint in the Ward on Branch Six, he'd been discharged and allowed to return to work. "Fallen from a great height," he told the Major, which technically wasn't a lie.

Initially, the injury had slumped him into a depressive state. Self-loathing seeped into his psyche. He grew frustrated spending his days watching wild birds zip about freely in the Outside World whilst he was stuck in the Watchtower, nursing a damaged wing, unable to improve his technique, therefore delaying any potential escape. Then one day, when watching a flock of geese return from their winter migration in a perfect V-formation, an inspired thought occurred to him. Whilst incapacitated and prevented from the practical aspects of flying, he would instead delve into the theoretical. From that point on he decided to use his time as a Lookout Guard more productively, utilising his position as an opportunity to study the mechanics of flight.

Puck became obsessed. A keen student with a lot of spare time, he dedicated his waking hours to researching the movement of birds, trying to understand the methodologies of maintaining airborne stability. He'd isolate a particular species and meticulously follow their manoeuvres. Starting with pigeons, he observed their explosive take off: the hyper-extension of legs pushing off in tandem with wings raised above its head, then the forced downwards thrust to create a vertical lift. He deduced that ducks have curved, pointed wings with a relatively short span, thus require continuous flapping to remain airborne, generally in a consistent trajectory. Sparrows use a bounding style with an irregular rhythm of rapid wingbeats followed by short swooping glides, whilst the tail frantically pumps up and down to provide stability and direction like a rudder. He became so well-versed in wild birds that without even looking, he could tell the difference between sounds of flight. Pigeons had a fluttery resonance to their flap, like whispers echoing along a tunnel. Ducks displayed a more stereotypical 'beat' noise, like a flag lapping against the wind. Sparrows were silent.

He had also stumbled on an interesting practice. At night, lying in his nest, he closed his eyes and using the power of imagination 'pretended' to fly. He visualised soaring over fictional landscapes — forests, deserts, oceans.

One time he even flew to the moon and back! Immersed in the experience, he envisaged what fresh air felt like on his beak as he coursed through the sky. He invoked the sensation of sun on his feathers. He tasted freedom. This experiment began as a bit of fun, escapism, something to take his mind off the pain, but over time it developed into something far more potent, especially when combined with physical movements. With eyes shut and imagination firing, he imitated the motions of the wild birds, flapping his wings and pivoting his tail, steering in synchronised gestures. This combination was sensorily powerful. It felt as if he could truly fly.

Memories came flooding back, nostalgic sensations deeply suppressed. When he was a chick, Puck used to play make-believe in this way all the time but soon grew out of it as society placed no value on such trivial matters. *Wings are for working.* Guided by blind intuition and fuelled by an insatiable desire to be free, he continued this practice every night until he fell into a deep sleep and dwelt in the realm of dreams.

Summer faded into autumn. Days drew shorter and nights grew longer, which meant less time working and more time playing. Puck had nearly made a full recovery. His damaged wing was still a little limp, but it was getting stronger every day, and he was on the up. He'd even gotten a promotion. Major Gruber had overheard him reciting the landing procedures of pigeons and, mistaking these insights for preventative measures against invasion, had decided he was ready to rise to the rank of sergeant. It meant more responsibility and a bigger box to maintain, but the extra ration of feed was most welcome. Puck was more interested in breaking out. His attention switched from studying flight to methods of escape. He'd mapped out every corner of Avalona, and at night he snuck about attempting different approaches. He tried chewing through the bars, but they proved too resilient. He considered digging his way out but soon gave up after trying to drill through concrete. He even followed the flow of rainwater as it disappeared down the drains but couldn't squeeze through the slits or lift the grill.

The parrot was running out of ideas. He was perched in the Watchtower, pretending to work, eyes closed and praying to a divine dodo he didn't believe in, seeking guidance, hoping for a sign, when he heard a loud bang.

The Featherless One had entered Avalona, and the door had flung back and landed flush against the wall. It clicked. Of course. As he stared at the gaping hole, it occurred to him that at any point any parrot could leave should they muster the courage and compulsion to do so. The Featherless One began the rounds whilst Puck dithered on his Lookout Perch caught between two minds: fight or flight. He didn't feel ready for an escape, but the open door looked so inviting. A gateway to a whole new world.

The Featherless One drew level with the Watchtower. For a moment they locked eyes. Puck felt overcome with guilt for even entertaining the idea of escape. But as they continued staring into each other his contrition was soon replaced with a realisation that this creature was no loyal servant: it was their captor. The Featherless One broke eye contact and went on its way. With little time to lose, Puck sprang into action. He leapt outside the Watchtower and clung onto Branch Two with purpose. Adrenaline pumping, he teetered on the edge and stared at the concrete floor way down below, which was a mistake. His lurching stomach twisted like a wrung dishcloth. Vertigo rocked his orientation. Paralysing doubt flooded through his body. "What am I doing?" he cried. "This is crazy". Perched on the precipice, he was about to throw away a promising career and potentially sacrifice his life. And for what?

Overwhelmed by fear, he looked around Avalona to see if anybody was watching, but they were all preoccupied, their gaze fixed on the feed. Slowly Puck stepped away from the edge. He wished to return to his comfortable enslavement, simply slip back inside the Watchtower, lick his tail, and pretend nothing had happened. But something fixed him to the spot. A force willing him forward. The voice of intuition. *This is your moment*. The bird stood firm, digging in his claws. Just as he'd practised hundreds of times, Puck bent his knees and raised his wings in a cruciform pose. He closed his eyes, and, in the domains of imagination, went through the motions, beginning a flap from the centre of the wing then rippling outwards to the tips with a whipped flick. He repeated this process several times, growing in confidence. He began to *believe*. Standing tall, he opened his bill and drew an extended breath to calm himself. Then, on the exhale, Puck took one final leap of faith.

And fell.

The feeling was like a sliding-door opening from beneath his feet, a sudden sinking sensation. Then gravity took grip. Freefalling, he flailed about like a person thrown into the deep end who can't swim. He flapped desperately, but his floundering wings couldn't get any purchase on the ether. There was no traction, no thrust. Gaining momentum, he plunged faster, harder, panicking, flapping, clutching, trying to grab hold of a branch or some rope but it was no use. He hurtled towards the concrete floor and certain death and was about to splat onto the ground when a primordial survival instinct kicked in and the bird arched his wings into a fulcrum, catching the air like a sail catching wind. His trajectory changed at the last moment, and he shot up like a rocket. Whoosh!

"I'm flying!" he cried. "I'M FLYINGGGGG!!"

The Avalonians broke rank to witness this unprecedented phenomenon unfolding before them. Some looked on open-beaked, whilst others blinked and rubbed their eyes in disbelief. *No, it cannot be! Wings are for working.* They watched as Puck flew round and round in circles, unaccustomed to this new system of navigation and unsure where to go or what to do with himself. He'd intended to make a beeline for the exit but got carried away, unable to stop circling the cage until he became dizzy, so landed on top of the tree. He took a moment to compose himself whilst his heart pounded into his skull.

"Ladies and gentlemen, birds of a feather," he announced to the enclosure, his voice breathless and nervous. The residents craned their necks to catch a glimpse, giddy with the collective excitement of when something spontaneous breaks the spell of routine. Queen Bola appeared on her Royal Perch, watching apprehensively. This wasn't the first time under her rule that a parrot had dared to escape. "Fellow citizens," he continued, "bear witness to the truth that lies within you, for we have been bred into a lie. Hatched in bondage. Raised in captivity. This place we call home is nothing more than a prison for parrots. And we are slaves!" The crowd broke into gasps and conspiratorial whispers. Queen Bola summoned her Patrol Guards at the ready. Oblivious, The Featherless One continued refilling feeders whilst humming its tune. Puck pressed on, projecting his voice. "Avalona is an artificial simulation of reality based on concepts and symbols. Everything you've ever known to be true is a fabrication designed to coerce you into obedience through mechanisms of fear. Those bars do not protect us from birds coming in. Their purpose is to prevent us from getting out! To stop us from living a rich life where we belong — the Outside World." He pointed a wing at the wilderness. "A place where we can do whatever we want with no rules or regulations. A place where we can eat as much food as we like without taxes. A place where we can fly freely with no jobs or responsibilities—"

"Heretic!" came a shout from the crowd.

"Blasphemy!" cried another.

"Traitor!"

The heckles knocked Puck off stride. This wasn't going to plan. In his rehearsals, the Avalonians were supposed to rise in numbers and follow him into the Promised Land. Instead, the crowd had become a mob. They were booing and hissing as if he were a pantomime villain. "Throw him in the Coop!" they chanted, "Throw him in the Coop!" Always willing to seize a favourable opportunity for public relations, Queen Bola gave the throat-slitting signal. On command, a squadron of Patrol Guards began scaling the tree in pursuit. The cage went wild, demanding blood. Puck stood frozen in shock as the advancing Patrol Guards closed in. Having just tasted flight and not fancying a lifetime locked up in the Coop, he launched off the branch just in time, slipping through their clutches. He flicked his wings as if touched by a wand and magically took flight, sailing through the open door without looking back.

He'd done it. He'd passed through the portal and made it to the other side. Freedom.

Gliding. Floating. Drifting. The wonder of flight was better than any of his wildest dreams or desires. Like levitating, the weightless sensation so liberating. Once fully clear of the cage and the life he'd left behind, Puck ripped the tag from his leg and spat it out defiantly. He took a big gulp of fresh air and felt the breeze on his beak, then stretched out his wings and tested the extent of his new abilities. He swirled around in barrel rolls and loop-de-loops, then switched gears into full-throttle mode, soaring higher and higher through the boundless expanse of sky before disappearing into nebulous clouds, never to be seen again.

After receiving a first-class degree in Creative
Writing at the Arts University Bournemouth,
Steve moved down the south coast to complete
postgraduate studies at the University of Plymouth.
He submitted several versions of *Spread Your Wings*
on various modules, including as a dissertation.
Every professor, however, discouraged Steve from
'wasting his time' writing about a parrot, and
instead focus his attention on more important
matters, such as 'postmodernism' or something.
This is Steve Dumar's debut book, about a parrot.

IF YOU LIKED THIS
BOOK PLEASE GIVE IT
A POSITIVE REVIEW

First Published in the United Kingdom in 2023
Copyright © 2023 by Steven Dumar

Book Design by Adam Hay Studio

ISBN: 978-1-7392869-0-3

Printed in Great Britain
by Amazon